ELEPHANT JOE is a Knight!

A tale of knightly chivalrousness

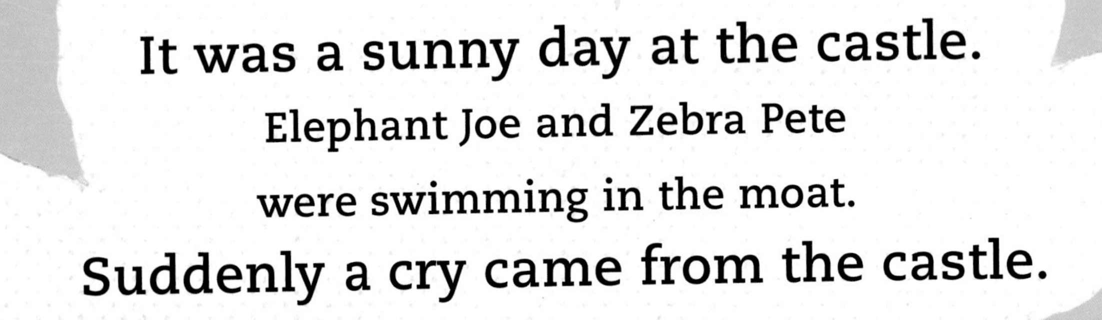

It was a sunny day at the castle.
Elephant Joe and Zebra Pete
were swimming in the moat.
Suddenly a cry came from the castle.

"Help!
Help!"
Does someone need
Elephant Joe's help?

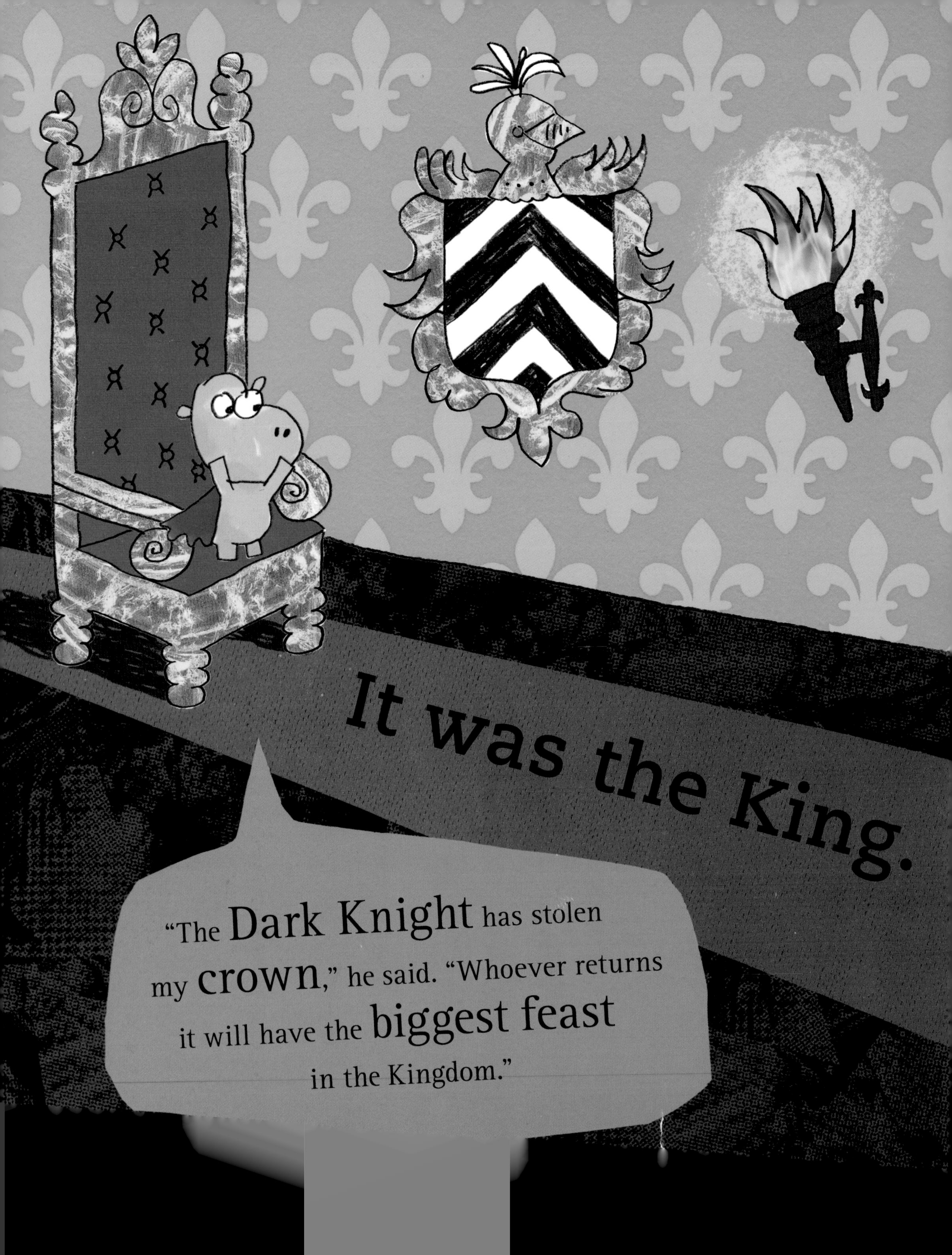
It was the King.
"The Dark Knight has stolen my crown," he said. "Whoever returns it will have the biggest feast in the Kingdom."

"Quick!" said Elephant Joe.
"We need armour!
We need horses!"

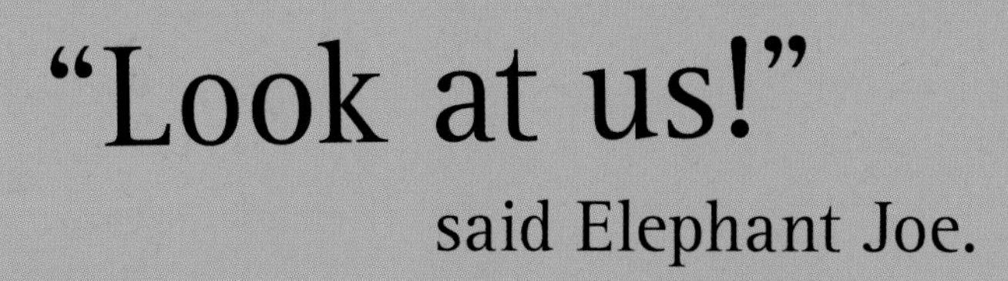

"Look at us!"
said Elephant Joe.
"We're knights!
We shall fight the Dark Knight
and rescue the King's crown.
Giddy up!"

They set off straight away.

Soon they were in the
Enchanted
Forest.

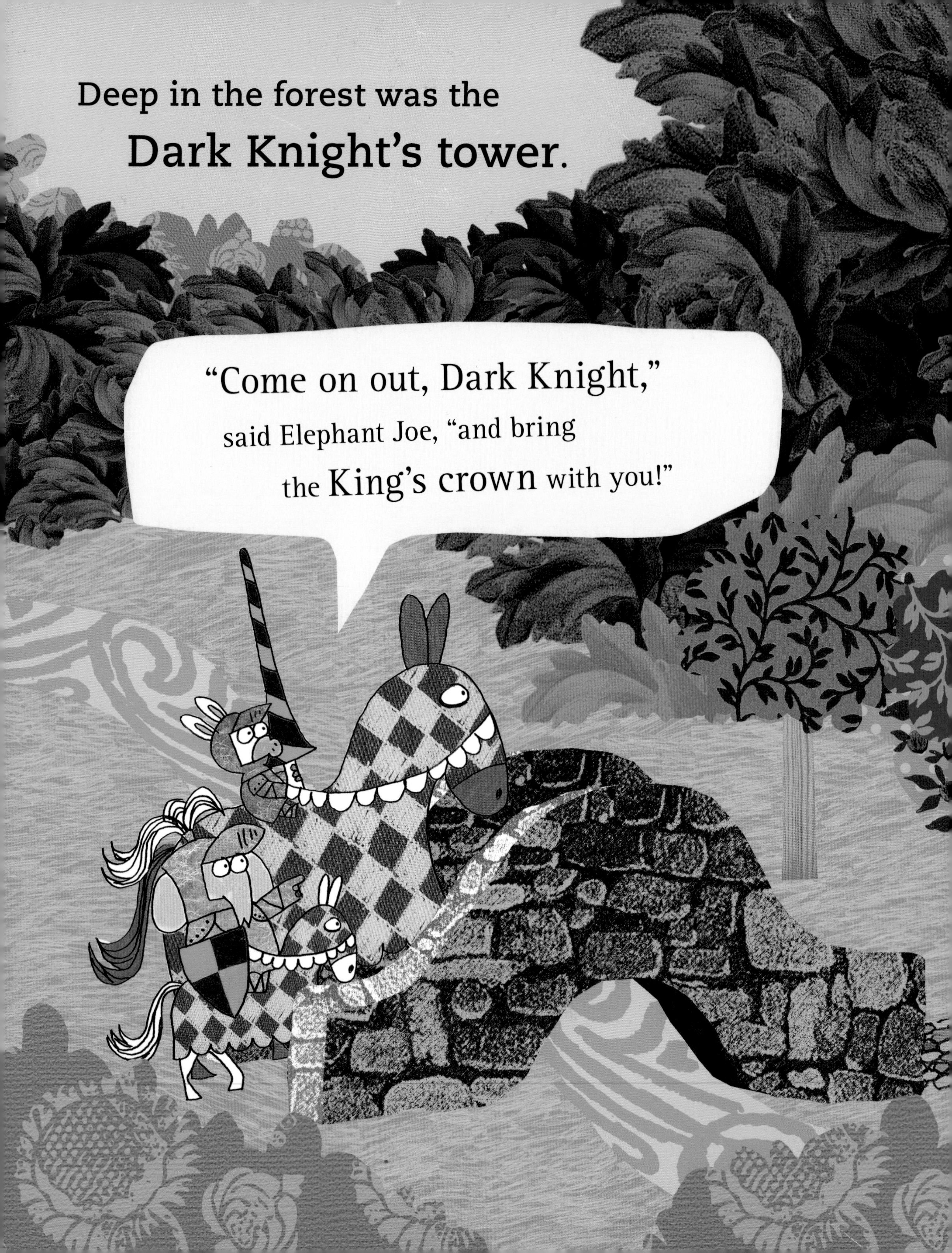
Deep in the forest was the
Dark Knight's tower.
"Come on out, Dark Knight,"
said Elephant Joe, "and bring
the King's crown with you!"

"The Dark Knight's not in," said a voice. "I'm just a damsel in distress."
Fear not, damsel. Elephant Joe will rescue you!

Suddenly there was a
terrible **roar**.
"Jumping jesters!"
said Elephant Joe. "We've
woken the dreaded dragon!
Back, you beast!"
ROAR

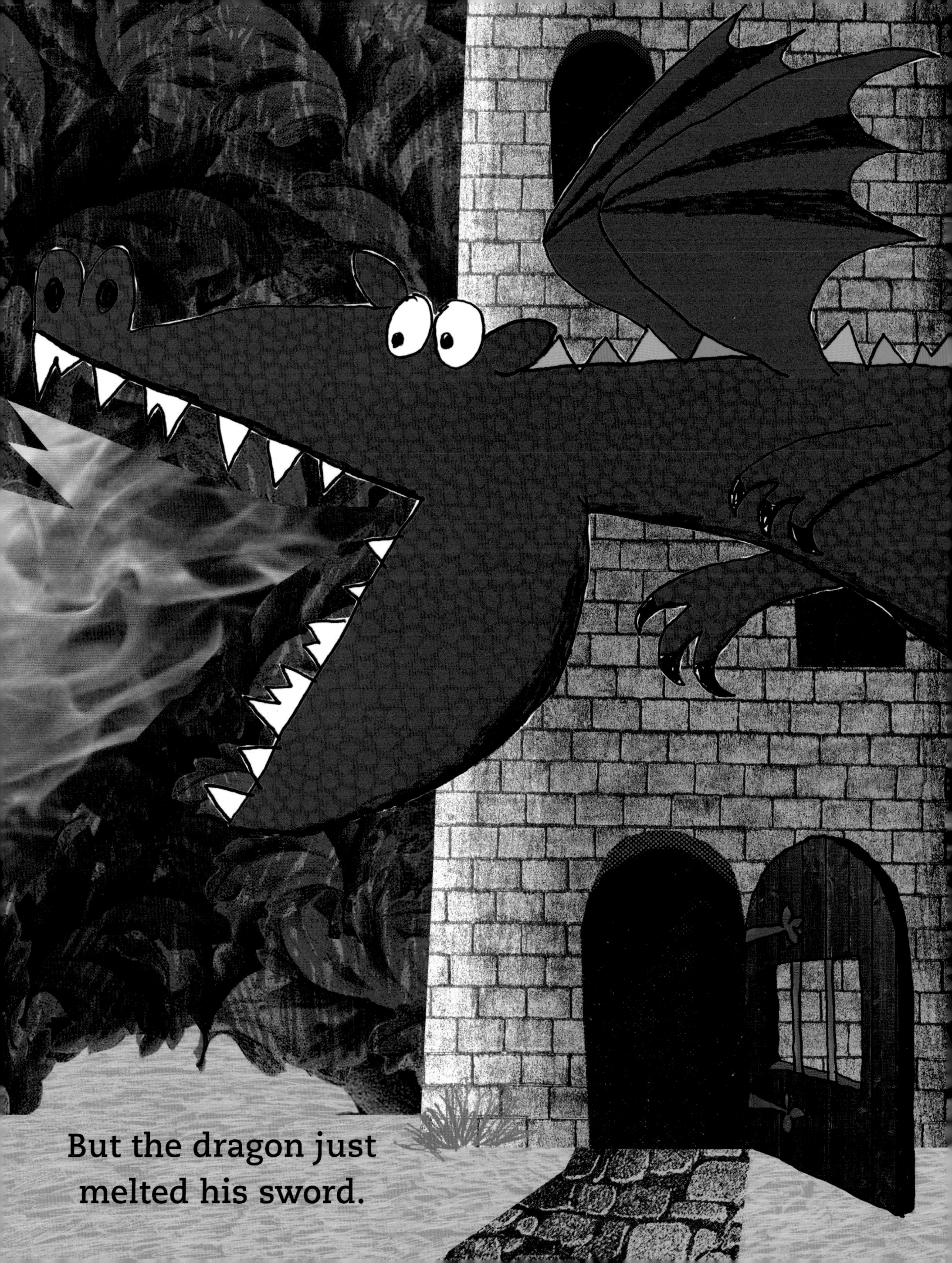

But the dragon just
melted his sword.

"Quick, Zebra Pete!"
said Elephant Joe.
"Joust with him!"

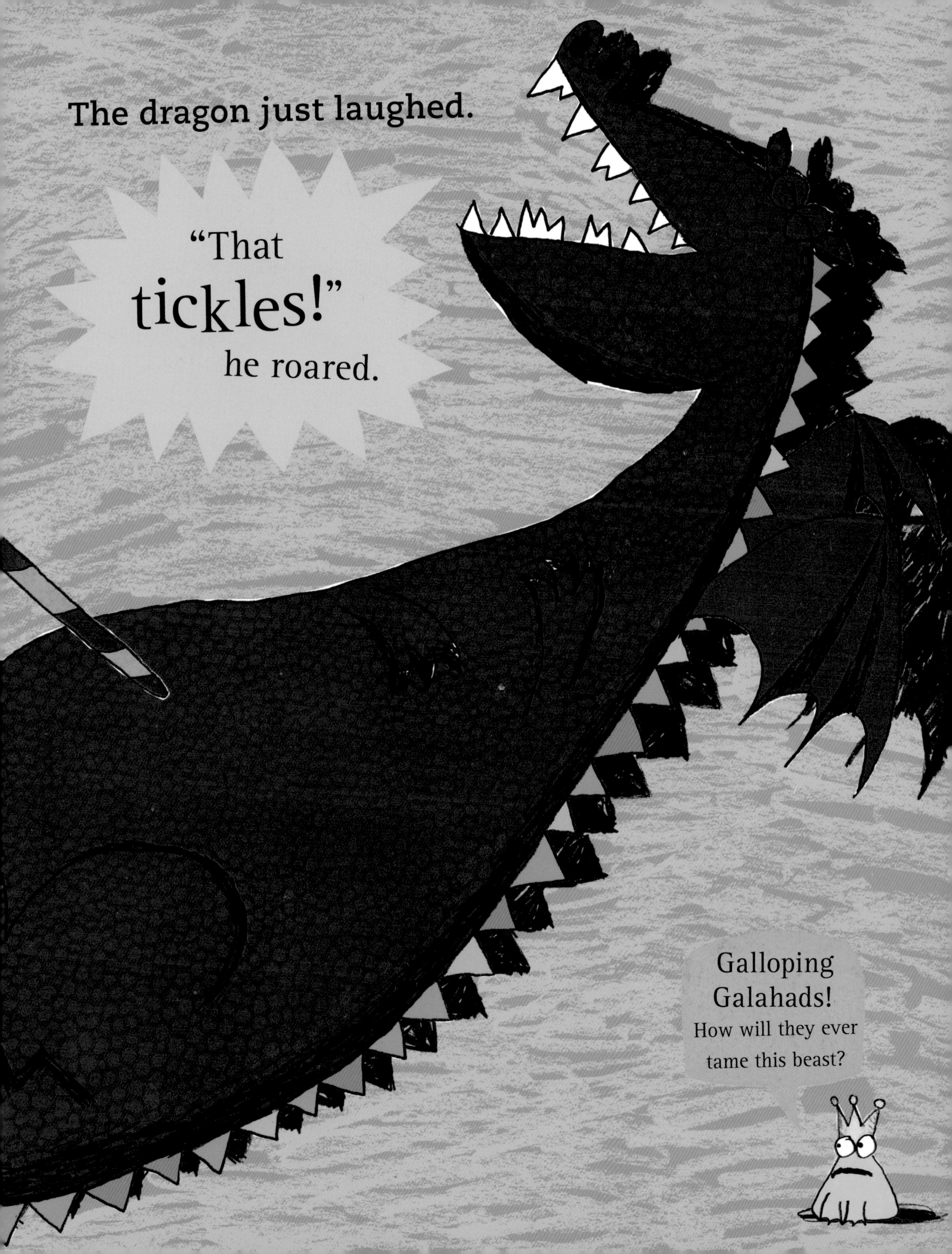
The dragon just laughed.
"That tickles!" he roared.
Galloping Galahads! How will they ever tame this beast?

Then Zebra Pete said:

No one had ever said "please" before.

He let them past.

"We're coming, damsel!" said Elephant Joe.
I hope this isn't a trick.

"Fair damsel! You are rescued!" said Elephant Joe.

But the damsel was . . .

The Dark Knight locked them in her tower.
Then she stole Zebra Pete's horse
and rode away!
"Ha-ha!" she laughed.
"Now I'm going to be
King of the Castle!"

Luckily, the dragon had a spare key.
He let them out . . .

. . . and gave them a lift.

"There she is!"
said Elephant Joe.
"Quick! Head for
the castle!"
ENCHANTED FOREST

They arrived just in time.

As the drawbridge went up, the horse chucked the Dark Knight into the moat. **Splosh!** went the crown into the water.

Luckily Elephant Joe was
an excellent swimmer.
"Stand back!"
he said.
"I shall rescue
the King's crown."

Quick as a flash,
he dived into
the moat.

He saved the
crown and
dragged the
Dark Knight
ashore.

The King was very pleased
to have his crown back.

Then the King said:
"Dark Knight, you have been very bad. How shall we punish you?"

"Make her **kiss** that frog," said Sir Elephant Joe.

Oh, yuck!

Yippee!
That'll turn me into a handsome prince!

"Good idea," said the King. "But first . . .

. . . let us have our feast!”
Can someone pass the flies, please?

"I like being a knight,"
said Sir Elephant Joe.

To Joe and Zack, from Great Uncle David

First published in the UK in 2011 by Alison Green Books
An imprint of Scholastic Children's Books
Euston House, 24 Eversholt Street, London NW1 1DB, UK
A division of Scholastic Ltd
www.scholastic.co.uk
London – New York – Toronto – Sydney – Auckland
Mexico City – New Delhi – Hong Kong

ISBN HB: 978 1 407115 57 3
ISBN PB: 978 1 407115 60 3

Printed in Singapore

10 9 8 7 6 5 4 3 2 1

Papers used by Scholastic Children's Books
are made from wood grown in sustainable forests.